for Sebastian with all my love

'de te fabula narratur'

First published 1992 by
Walker Books Ltd, 87 Vauxhall Walk
London SE11 5HJ

This edition published 1994

2 4 6 8 10 9 7 5 3 1

This book has been typeset in ITC Garamond Light.

Printed in Hong Kong

British Library Cataloguing in Publication Data
A catalogue record for this book is available from the British Library.

ISBN 0-7445-3125-X

THIS WALKER BOOK BELONGS TO:

_____

When I'm BIG

Debi Gliori

FALKIRK COUNCIL
LIBRARY SUPPORT
FOR SCHOOLS

WALKER BOOKS
LONDON

When I'm big, I'm going to stay up as late as I like and make myself marshmallows on toast instead of going to bed.

When I'm big, I'm going swimming with the whales in the deep blue sea instead of puddling about in the bath.

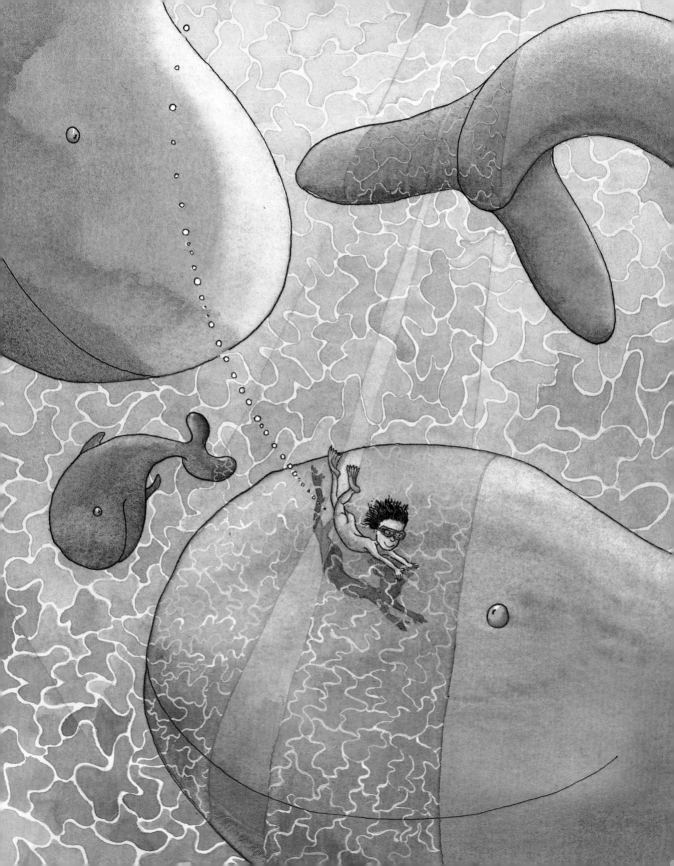

When I'm big,
I'm going to wear
a bird-suit and
gumboots all day
long instead of
a jumper and
dungarees.

When I'm big, I'm going to have a huge back garden with sand mountains that touch the sky and a lake in the middle instead of a sandpit and a paddling pool.

When I'm big,
I'm going to
drive the trolley
round the shops
with Dad in it
instead of the
other way round.

When I'm big,
I'm going to
grow triffids and
Venus fly-traps
and man-eating
orchids instead of
mustard and cress.

When I'm big I'm going to ride a proper bike instead of a tricycle.

When I'm big, I'm going to have twelve lions, two tigers, a bunch of grizzly bears and a shark instead of a dog, a cat and a goldfish.

When I'm big,
I'm going to put
Mum and Dad
to bed and read
them a story and
turn out the light
and go downstairs
on my own.

I can squeeze
into the safest
place in the world.

MORE WALKER PAPERBACKS
For You to Enjoy

Also by Debi Gliori

MY LITTLE BROTHER

Sometimes the little girl in this delightful story wishes
her bothersome little brother would just disappear –
until, one night, he does!

0-7445-3612-X   £3.99

NEW BIG SISTER

One moment Mum's off her food and the next
she's eating marmalade and cold spaghetti sandwiches!
What's going on? Mum's having a baby, of course. But the
biggest surprise is yet to come! Ideal for preparing
children for a new arrival.

0-7445-3610-3   £3.99

NEW BIG HOUSE

The hall is full of baby walkers, the kitchen is
bursting with laundry and the living room is a Lego minefield...
What the family in this lively book needs is a new big house.
But finding one proves to be a big headache!

0-7445-3609-X   £3.99

**Walker Paperbacks are available from most booksellers, or by post from
Walker Books Ltd, PO Box 11, Falmouth, Cornwall TR10 9EN.**

To order, send: Title, author, ISBN number and price for each book ordered, your full name and address, cheque or postal order
for the total amount, plus postage and packing: UK and BFPO Customers – £1.00 for first book, plus 50p for the second book
and plus 30p for each additional book to a maximum charge of £3.00. Overseas and Eire Customers – £2.00 for first book,
plus £1.00 for the second book and plus 50p per copy for each additional book.
Prices are correct at time of going to press, but are subject to change without notice.